For Lilly and Jacob
J. K.

For Marion and Bill
P.C.M.

First published in 1994 by Hamish Hamilton Ltd, London.
First published in the United States in 1994
by Hyperion Books for Children.

Printed in Hong Kong.
For information address
Hyperion Books for Children, 114 Fifth Avenue, New York, New York 10011.

FIRST EDITION
1 3 5 7 9 10 8 6 4 2

Library of Congress Cataloging-in-Publication Data
Koralek, Jenny.
Cat and Kit/Jenny Koralek; illustrated by Patricia MacCarthy — 1st ed.
p. cm.
Summary: Cat finds young Kit alone in the woods and takes
it upon himself to teach the kitten how to live in the wild.
ISBN 0-7868-0037-2 (trade) — ISBN 0-7868-2030-6 (lib. bdg.)
[1. Cats — Fiction.] I. MacCarthy, Patricia, ill. II. Title.
PZ7.K8363Cat 1995 [E]—dc20 94-6916 CIP AC

Cat & Kit

JENNY KORALEK

ILLUSTRATED BY PATRICIA MACCARTHY

Hyperion Books for Children
New York

Cat was old and Cat was wise.
He spoke without words,
he spoke with his eyes.
Cat watched the wild and hunted for
his food and protected his own.

Cat walked alone as most cats do.
He walked through the woods
and over the fields
and around the farm.
Cat watched the wild and hunted for his food and
protected his own.

Mouse and Rat were terrified of Cat, and
so was Rabbit.
Cat was terrified of no one, not even of Fox or Badger.
Cat watched the wild and hunted for his food and
protected his own.

One day in the woods Cat came upon a sad sight:
one small Kit,
meow,
meow,
meow.
One small Kit not ready for the wild, not ready to hunt for his food and protect his own.

But Cat knew what to do.
He took Kit between his teeth and
dropped him at the farmer's door.

Farmer picked up Kit and stroked him with gentle fingers.

"Wise Cat!" said Farmer. "He knows I will feed Kit with Cow's warm milk. He knows I will give him good scraps from my table when Kit's teeth grow sharp."

Cat watched and waited for many days till Kit's
legs were sturdy and his whiskers long.
And then one night Cat came for Kit and took him
through the woods and over the fields and around the farm.
Kit killed Mouse and Cat killed Rat, and, together, with
heads and tails held high, they walked past Fox and Badger.
This is the wild, said Cat to Kit with unblinking eyes.
This is where you will hunt for your food
and protect your own.

But the next day, in the afternoon, when Cat was sleeping, Farmer put a ribbon around Kit's neck and gave him as a birthday present to his grandson, who lived in a house on a street in the town.
No woods, no fields, no farm, no mice, no rats, no rabbits. No owl, no fox, no badger.
And no Cat.

But a cushion for Kit on a special chair, and a dish for Kit, and food from a can, and cars to dodge, and dogs to dodge, and stones underfoot to hurt the paws, and puzzling balls of string pulled this way and that by a little boy.
This is not the wild, said Kit's sad eyes. Oh no, this is not the wild. Here I will never hunt for my food or protect my own.

Farmer's grandson heard Kit's unspoken words.
He took Kit in his arms and untied the ribbon.
He climbed on a bus and took Kit home through
the woods and over the fields and around the farm.

Farmer's grandson stroked Kit twice and put him down by Cat.
"I'm letting him go," said the boy.
We must both let him go, said Cat without words.
"Wise Cat, wise boy," said Farmer.